For Sophie and Hannah

Originally published under the title
Ophelia by Lemniscaat b.v. Rotterdam, 2008
Printed in Belgium
First U.S. edition, 2009

ISBN-13: 978-1-59078-659-8

CIP data is available

Lemniscaat
An Imprint of Boyds Mills Press, Inc.
815 Church Street
Honesdale, Pennsylvania 18431

Ingrid & Dieter Schubert

Ophelia

Lemniscaat

Honesdale, Pennsylvania

One beautiful morning, Ophelia woke up.
She lay back and stretched.

"Oh, Ophelia ..." came a voice from afar.

Ophelia looked up. It was Kevin's voice.

"Where are you?" shouted Ophelia. "And why are you yelling like that?"

"Oh ...," Kevin said again. "I don't know what to do! I have all these butterflies in my stomach."

"Kevin is ill," Ophelia thought. "He needs my help."
"Where are you running off to?" Meerkat asked.
"Kevin screamed something about having stomachaches. He didn't sound very well."

"I have stomachaches all the time," Meerkat said. "You know what helps? A hot-water bottle. Wait, I'll go with you."

"What's wrong with Kevin?" Frog asked.

"He has a terrible cramp. And his throat hurts."

"Ah, then he should drink some herbal tea."

"Where are you going?" Porcupine asked.

"We're going to find Kevin. He has pains everywhere and can hardly speak. I think he must have fallen out of a tree."

"Poor Kevin!" Porcupine screamed. "Will he ever be able to walk again?"

"What's wrong? What's wrong?" asked Rhino.

"Kevin fell out of a tree and broke his leg. He's in a lot of pain and can't move anymore."

"I'm coming with you," said Rhino. He hurried out of the water.

"What's all that noise?" Toucan yelled. "Where's the fire?"
"No fire! Haven't you heard about Kevin?"

"Kevin has been in a terrible accident!
He broke all of his bones!" cried Rhino.

"What's going on here?" Turtle wanted to know.
Toucan cawed. "Kevin is dead," he screeched.
"DEAD?" yelled Meerkat, Frog, Porcupine, and Rhino.

They sat down at the bank, feeling very sad.

Kevin, dead? What had happened? And where was Ophelia?

Had she heard the terrible news?

"Hello!" came a happy voice. And there was Ophelia, with Kevin!
"What! You're not dead at all?" they yelled.
"Of course not," said Kevin. "Who said I was?"

"What was wrong with you, then?" Rhino asked.

"He was just a little nervous about being in love," laughed Ophelia.

"Does being in love kill you?" asked Frog.

"No," Toucan said. "But it sure is contagious."